The BOBBSEY TWINS®

Freddie and Flossie

by Laura Lee Hope

illustrated by Chuck Pyle

Ready-to-Read
Aladdin
New York   London   Toronto   Sydney

Visit us at www.abdopub.com

Spotlight, a division of ABDO Publishing Company, is a school and library distributor of high quali
reinforced library bound editions.

Library bound edition © 2006

Library of Congress Cataloging-in-Publication Data

Hope, Laura Lee.
Freddie and Flossie / by Laura Lee Hope; illustrated by Chuck Pyle.—1st ed.
p. cm.—(Ready-to-Read) (Bobbsey twins)
Summary: Twins Freddie and Flossie play at having a store and at being firefighters.
1-4169-0270-8 (pbk.)
[1. Twins—Fiction. 2. Brothers and sisters—Fiction. 3. Play—Fiction.]
I. Pyle, Chuck, 1954- ill. II. Title. III. Series.
PZ7.H772Fp 2005
[E]—dc22 2004017888
1-59961-095-7 (reinforced library bound edition)

All Spotlight books are reinforced library binding and manufactured in the United States of Americ

Meet Freddie and Flossie.

They are twins.

They have blond hair.

They have blue eyes.

Freddie is loud.

Flossie is not.

Freddie plays firefighter.

CLANG! CLANG!

Flossie plays store.

May I help you?

Fire! Fire!

Have a nice day.

Here comes Freddie.

No!

Freddie is a good firefighter.

Here comes Flossie.

She is a good firefighter too!